Welcome to ALADDIN QUIX!

If you are looking for fast, fun-to-read stories with colorful characters, lots of kid-friendly humor, easy-to-follow action, entertaining story lines, and lively illustrations, then **ALADDIN QUIX** is for you!

But wait, there's more!

If you're also looking for stories with tables of contents; word lists; about-the-book questions; 64, 80, or 96 pages; short chapters; short paragraphs; and large fonts, then **ALADDIN QUIX** is *definitely* for you!

ALADDIN QUIX: The next step between ready to reads and longer, more challenging chapter books, for readers five to eight years old.

Read more ALADDIN QUIX books!

A Miss Mallard Mystery
By Robert Quackenbush

A Miss Mallard Mystery

STAGE DOOR TO TERROR

ROBERT QUACKENBUSH

ALADDIN QUIX

New York London Toronto Sydney New Delhi

ALADDIN QUIX
Simon & Schuster Children's Publishing Division
1230 Avenue of the Americas, New York, New York 10020
This Aladdin QUIX paperback edition January 2020
Copyright © 1985 by Robert Quackenbush
Also available in an Aladdin QUIX hardcover edition.
All rights reserved, including the right of reproduction in whole or in part in any form.
ALADDIN and the related marks and colophon are registered
trademarks of Simon & Schuster, Inc.
For information about special discounts for bulk purchases, please contact
Simon & Schuster Special Sales at 1-866-506-1949 or business@simonandschuster.com.
The Simon & Schuster Speakers Bureau can bring authors to your live event. For
more information or to book an event contact the Simon & Schuster Speakers Bureau
at 1-866-248-3049 or visit our website at www.simonspeakers.com.
Designed by Tiara Iandiorio
The illustrations for this book were rendered in pen and ink and wash.
The text of this book was set in Archer Medium.
Manufactured in the United States of America 1219 OFF
2 4 6 8 10 9 7 5 3 1
Library of Congress Control Number 2019936829
ISBN 978-1-5344-1409-9 (hc)
ISBN 978-1-5344-1408-2 (pbk)
ISBN 978-1-5344-1410-5 (eBook)

First for Piet

and now for Emma and Aidan

Cast of Characters

Miss Mallard: World-famous ducktective

Willard Widgeon: Miss Mallard's nephew, and inspector for the Swiss police

Claudine Pilet: Performer and granddaughter of Lily Pilet

Lily Pilet: Famous singer and dancer, and friend of Miss Mallard

Monsieur Carrot: Manager of the Canard-Rouge

Marie: Claudine's assistant

Helene Eider: Friend of Marie

Gerard Tadorne: Stage doorman at the Canard-Rouge

Georgette: Flower seller at the Eiffel Tower

Pierre: Headwaiter

Philippe Souchet: Waiter at the Canard-Rouge

Officer Goldeneye: Parisian police officer

What's in Miss Mallard's Bag?

Miss Mallard has many detective tools she brings with her on her adventures around the world.

In her knitting bag she usually has:

- Newspaper clippings
- Knitting needles and yarn
- A magnifying glass
- A flashlight
- A mirror
- A travel guide
- Chocolates for her nephew

Contents

1

Ducknapped!

On a weekend tour of Paris, **Miss Mallard**—the world-famous ducktective—was joined by her nephew, **Willard Widgeon** of the Swiss police.

They especially wanted to see

Claudine Pilet, who was going to sing and dance at a night-club called the Canard-Rouge. Claudine was the granddaughter of an old family friend, **Lily Pilet**.

"Isn't this exciting, Willard?" asked Miss Mallard as they sat down at a table near the stage.

"Just ducky!" said Inspector Widgeon.

A waiter took their orders and returned with two pots of tea.

Inspector Widgeon raised his

cup and said, **"Here's to Claudine!"**

"And may her success be as bright as her grandmother's," said Miss Mallard.

"I met Lily Pilet many years ago. She was the toast of Paris in her day. She was often **courted** by royalty," she added.

"It was even rumored that a wealthy king had **showered** her with gifts of priceless diamonds, rubies, and emeralds!

"True or not, she was greatly

loved by everyone and sadly missed when she retired from the stage.

"But just imagine!" Miss Mallard continued. "After all these years, Claudine is stepping into Lily's costumes and **re-creating** her songs and dances at the famous Canard-Rouge."

Just then the cancan dancers finished their dancing. The lights dimmed and a hush came over the audience.

"Shhhhhhh!"

The music began and Claudine stepped onstage.

Everyone in the crowd **oohed and aahed**!

Never before had they seen such a glittering, shimmering, sparkling costume.

"Willard," whispered Miss Mallard, "she looks just like Lily did when she was young. And the program says that she is going to perform Lily's spectacular 'Rain of Light' dance."

"I can't wait," Willard answered.

But, **oh no!** As soon as she started to sing, someone came swinging out onto the stage on a rope. He was wearing a mask. He grabbed Claudine and **scooped** her off the stage.

The audience was horrified. Everyone quacked loudly.

"Good heavens, Aunty!" cried Inspector Widgeon in alarm. "Claudine has been ducknapped!"

At once, the manager, **Monsieur Carrot**, rushed out onto the stage to quiet the audience.

"Keep on playing! Keep on dancing!" he shouted to the orchestra and the performers.

"Let's go, Willard!" said Miss Mallard. "We will pay our waiter later!" They made a **hasty** exit.

Outside, they went down a narrow alley until they came to the stage door. Opening it, they didn't see a stage doorman, so they continued on their way.

Backstage, everyone was racing around looking for Claudine.

It was a sea of **confusion**.

They looked behind curtains, behind scenery, in the cellar, and in the **rafters**.

Twenty minutes later someone cried, "Quick! Here, in the attic! **Claudine has been found!**"

Miss Mallard and Inspector Widgeon ran up a **spiral** staircase to the attic. They got there just as Claudine was being rescued by one of the stagehands.

The masked ducknapper was nowhere in sight!

2

Hidden Jewels

Monsieur Carrot burst into the dusty attic behind Miss Mallard and Inspector Widgeon.

"Claudine, my star, are you all right?" asked the club manager.

"I *will* be as soon as I pull myself together," answered Claudine.

She caught her breath and added, "I want to go on with the show. But give me half an hour before I do. I can't imagine who wanted to mess up my act. He just brought me up here and left by the open window. What a strange duck!"

"I'm glad you weren't harmed," said Monsieur Carrot. "I'll tell the audience that your act will be delayed. Take your time."

Miss Mallard and Inspector Widgeon followed Claudine to her dressing room. When Claudine opened the door, she let out a gasp.

OH NO!

Everything was a mess!

"Who did this?" cried Claudine. "And who left this flower here?"

She went over to her dressing table and picked up a single red carnation.

"I think I know," said Inspector Widgeon. "The carnation is the **trademark** of the Red Carnation, a **notorious** international jewel thief. He has left red carnations all over Italy, Switzerland, and Germany. So now he is in Paris! If we could only find out who he is and catch him!"

"Whoever he is," said Miss Mallard, "I believe he was not working alone. It looks like he had a partner ducknap Claudine. Then, while everyone was looking for her, he robbed the dressing room."

"But, why me? **I have no jewels!**" said Claudine. "And nothing is missing!"

She thought for a moment, and she said, "I know! Grandmother sent me a copy of her 'Rain of Light' costume this morning.

"She had sent me the *real* one a few days ago," she explained. "But then she was worried something might happen to it. She asked me to store the costume in a safe place until she could pick it up.

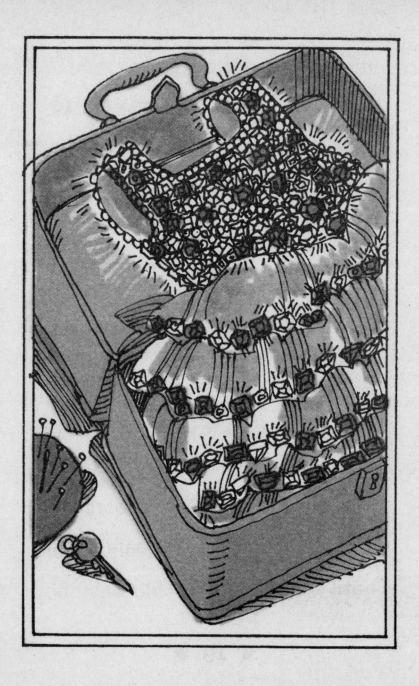

"**Marie**, my assistant, packed it in a suitcase and checked it at a railroad station for **safekeeping**. Then she sewed the **claim ticket** into the **hem** of my skirt. Do you suppose that is what the thief was looking for?"

"**Aha!**" Miss Mallard blurted out. "I bet he was looking for the king's jewels. So the story about Lily receiving royal gifts was true! And she had them sewn onto her costume to keep them very safe. No one would imagine that her costume had *real* jewels on it."

"No one, that is, but the Red Carnation thief," said Inspector Widgeon. "He can sniff out *real* jewels anywhere. And with two thieves on the job, it would be twice as easy."

"Quick, Claudine!" said Miss Mallard. "We must **retrieve** your suitcase before the thieves do. I'm sure they will put two and two together and realize that it has been checked."

3

Where Is Marie?

Claudine made a little tear in the hem of her costume. She carefully removed the claim ticket she had hidden there and handed it to Miss Mallard.

"Thank you," Miss Mallard said.

Miss Mallard looked at the ticket. It was torn at one corner. All that could be read was the word *"gare."* Below that was the number 44.

"'Gare' means station," said Miss Mallard. "But the rest of the name has been lost. Which station could it be? There are so many of them in Paris—not counting all the underground stations for the city's subways, called the Metro."

"Ooh-la-la," said Claudine. "Only Marie knows that answer.

And I gave her the evening off. We've got to find her!"

"Where could Marie be?" asked Miss Mallard.

"Well," said Claudine, "I know that she has a friend, **Helene Eider**, who works at the Notre Dame Cathedral."

"Let's go check it out, Willard," said Miss Mallard.

They went to the doorman **Gerard Tadorne**'s tiny glass office by the stage door. He called for a taxi.

When Miss Mallard and Inspector Widgeon got to Notre Dame, they pounded on a heavy wooden door. Helene Eider opened it for the two ducktectives. They told her why they were there.

"Marie was here earlier," said Helene Eider. "Then she went to see **Georgette**, who sells flowers at the Eiffel Tower."

"Let's go, Willard!" said Miss Mallard.

"Wouldn't it be best for me to go back and question the cancan

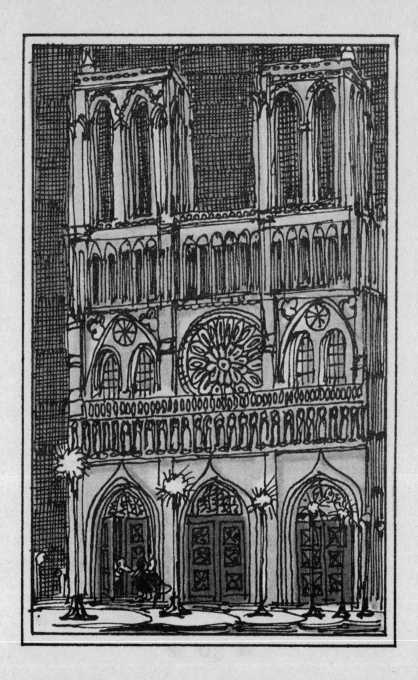

dancers, Aunty?" asked Inspector Widgeon.

"No, Willard," said Miss Mallard **firmly**.

They took the subway to the Eiffel Tower. Georgette was out front selling flowers.

"Marie *just* left," Georgette told them. "She said that she was going to the Café du Nantes in Montmartre to see her friend **Pierre**, who works there. Here, have a flower."

"Thank you," said Miss Mallard.

They took another train to Montmartre—the artists' section of Paris. They found the Café du Nantes on one of the side streets. Pierre, they discovered, was the headwaiter there. He took them to a table at the back of the café.

There sat Marie!

Miss Mallard told Marie why they had come looking for her.

"I checked the suitcase at the Gare de Lyon," said Marie. "That's because I know the attendant at that station and trust him."

"We don't have a moment to waste. Thank you, Marie!" said Miss Mallard. She and Inspector Widgeon quickly left the café.

4

A Suitcase Switch

Outside, Miss Mallard said, "What if we were able to catch the thieves and retrieve Claudine's suitcase at the same time, Willard?"

"How?" asked Inspector Widgeon.

"Here's my plan," explained Miss Mallard. "First, take this key to my hotel room. Next, find my empty suitcase and put my knitting bag inside. Then, check the suitcase at the Gare de Lyon. Finally, take the claim ticket to Claudine and ask her to bring it with her to the station."

Willard took the key and Miss Mallard said, "I will meet her there and explain everything. You wait for us at a table near the stage at the Canard-Rouge."

One hour later, Miss Mallard stood hidden in a dark corner of the waiting room at the Gare de Lyon. At last, she saw Claudine come in and called to her.

"Were you followed?" asked Miss Mallard.

"Yes, I was," said Claudine. "What is this about?"

"I need your help, Claudine," said Miss Mallard. "You must go at once and claim my suitcase with the ticket that Willard gave you."

"But what about *my* suitcase?" asked Claudine.

"I still have the ticket for it," said Miss Mallard. "But first we've got to catch the thieves!"

5

To Catch a Thief

Claudine walked across the busy station to the baggage claim. She handed the attendant the ticket. After she collected Miss Mallard's suitcase, she quickly headed back to the waiting room.

She was halfway across the room when suddenly someone— *whoosh*—rushed at her from behind and grabbed the suitcase. The robber ran with it to the street exit.

"Help! Police!" cried Claudine.

A police officer came running.

Miss Mallard was waiting by the exit. She saw the robber about to jump into a waiting taxi.

"There he is, Officer!" she called.

Quick as lightning, the officer stopped the robber before he had a chance to make a getaway with the suitcase.

Claudine came out onto the street.

"I know him!" she cried. "He is **Philippe Souchet**! He is a waiter at the Canard-Rouge!"

"Right!" said Miss Mallard. "And his partner is inside the taxi."

Claudine looked inside the taxi.

"Gerard Tadorne—our stage doorman!" exclaimed Claudine.

"Yes," said Miss Mallard. "I wondered why a stage doorman *wasn't* on duty when Willard and I first went backstage. They stay at their post during an emergency. Confess, Gerard Tadorne! You were the ducknapper!"

"You've gone quackers!" said Gerard Tadorne. "The suitcase is ours, Officer."

"If what you say is true," said the officer, "what's inside it?"

"A costume," said Philippe. "A glittering one."

"That's right!" said Gerard. "A friend of ours asked us to claim it for her."

The police officer turned to Miss Mallard and Claudine and asked, "And what do you say?"

"*My* knitting bag is inside the suitcase," said Miss Mallard.

"*Hmm,*" said the police officer. "Let's take it to the stationmaster's office and see who is telling the truth."

6

Carnation on the Run

In the stationmaster's office, the police officer snapped open the suitcase and found...

"My knitting bag!" said Miss Mallard.

Gerard and Philippe ran.

"Hold it!" said

the police officer.

"We made a mistake," said Gerard. "We thought it was *our* suitcase."

"You are both under arrest, for attempting to **commit** a robbery," said the police officer. "I'm taking you to police headquarters."

"Be sure to take their feather-prints," said Miss Mallard. "I believe you'll find that Philippe's prints match the prints of the

international jewel thief called the Red Carnation."

The policeman took the crooks away.

"Good tip!" said the police officer as he took the crooks away. "I told you that this wild **scheme** of yours would never work."

"Humph!" said Philippe. "This is what I get for asking *you* to help. I should have done it myself."

Miss Mallard and Claudine watched them leave.

"How can I ever thank you, Miss Mallard?" said Claudine. "But is my suitcase with the real jeweled costume inside still safe?"

"Let's go and see," said Miss Mallard.

They went to the baggage claim and presented the ticket.

"That's it!" said Claudine. "That's my suitcase. And here's the key to open it. I've kept it on a chain around my neck."

They set the suitcase on a bench and opened it. Inside was

the costume covered with many sparkling jewels.

"Ooh-la-la!" said Claudine. "See how the jewels sparkle! Grandmother Lily will be so happy to hear that they are safe. I'm so grateful to you, Miss Mallard."

"It wouldn't have been possible without you," said Miss Mallard.

With that they left the station to go back to the Canard-Rouge in time for Claudine's next show.

Back at the club, Miss Mallard

went to find Inspector Widgeon to tell him that the case was solved.

He was backstage chatting with the cancan dancers, so Miss Mallard went out front to watch the show alone.

And then, who should she find at her table but the policeman who made the arrest!

"Hello, Miss Mallard. I'm **Officer Goldeneye**," he said. "I'm off duty now. I thought we could celebrate together."

"I would be pleased as punch," said Miss Mallard. "In fact, I think I'll have some—instead of my usual tea. **Cheers!**"

Word List

claim ticket (KLAYM TIK·et):
A small, narrow piece of paper
used to have someone return
luggage or belongings

commit (kuh·MIT): To do
something that is harmful or illegal

confusion (kuhn·FYOO·zhun):
A situation in which people are
uncertain or mixed up about
what to do

courted (KOR·ted): Gave a lot of
attention to someone

firmly (FURM·lee): Hold tightly

hasty (HAY·stee): Quick or fast

hem (HEM): The bottom edge of a dress, skirt, pants, or shirt

notorious (no·TOR·ee·us): Known or famous for doing something bad or negative

rafters (RAF·turs): Large, long pieces of wood that support a roof

re-creating (REE·kree·ATE·ing): Making something over again

retrieve (ree·TREEV): To bring or get back from a place

safekeeping (SAYF·KEEP·ing):
Protecting something from harm

scheme (SKEEM): A clever or
dishonest plan

scooped (SKOOPT): Picked up
someone or something

showered (SHAU·erd): Gave in
large amounts

spiral (SPY·ruhl): A curve that
circles around and around

trademark (TRAYD·mahrk): A
symbol or name that someone
uses to show who they are

Questions

1. Why was the international jewel thief called the Red Carnation?
2. At what Paris landmark does Georgette sell flowers?
3. What was the name of Lily Pilet's famous dance?
4. Where did Lily hide the king's jewels? Why?
5. What section in Paris is known as the artists' section?

Acknowledgments

My thanks and appreciation go to Jon Anderson, president and publisher of Simon & Schuster Children's Books, and his talented team: Karen Nagel, executive editor; Karin Paprocki, art director; Tiara Iandiorio, designer; Elizabeth Mims, production editor; Sara Berko, production manager; Tricia Lin, assistant editor; and Richard Ackoon, executive coordinator; for launching out into the world again these incredible new editions of my Miss Mallard Mystery books for today's young readers everywhere.

CHUCKLE YOUR WAY THROUGH THESE EASY-TO-READ ILLUSTRATED CHAPTER BOOKS!